PRAISE FOR M.

Tom Clancy fans open to a strong female lead will clamor for more.

— *DRONE*, PUBLISHERS WEEKLY

Superb!

— *DRONE*, BOOKLIST STARRED REVIEW

The best military thriller I've read in a very long time. Love the female characters.

— *DRONE*, SHELDON MCARTHUR, FOUNDER OF
THE MYSTERY BOOKSTORE, LA

A fabulous soaring thriller.

— *TAKE OVER AT MIDNIGHT*, MIDWEST BOOK
REVIEW

Meticulously researched, hard-hitting, and suspenseful.

— *PURE HEAT*, PUBLISHERS WEEKLY, STARRED
REVIEW

Expert technical details abound, as do realistic military missions with superb imagery that will have readers feeling as if they are right there in the midst and on the edges of their seats.

Buchman has catapulted his way to the top tier of my favorite authors.

Nonstop action that will keep readers on the edge of their seats.

M L. Buchman's ability to keep the reader right in the middle of the action is amazing.

The only thing you'll ask yourself is, "When does the next one come out?"

The first...of (a) stellar, long-running (military) romantic suspense series.

I knew the books would be good, but I didn't realize how good.

Buchman mixes adrenalin-spiking battles and brusque military jargon with a sensitive approach.

13 times "Top Pick of the Month"

CAVE RESCUE
COURTSHIP

A US COAST GUARD ROMANTIC SUSPENSE
STORY

M. L. BUCHMAN

Buchman Bookworks

SIGN UP FOR M. L. BUCHMAN'S NEWSLETTER TODAY

and receive:
Release News
Free Short Stories
a Free book

Get your free book today. Do it now.
free-book.mlbuchman.com

Other works by M. L. Buchman: (* - also in audio)

Other works by M. L. Buchman:

Short Story Series by M. L. Buchman:

ABOUT THIS BOOK

Petty Officer Vera Chu lives her dream of serving aboard a US Coast Guard cutter. Newly assigned to patrols of the treacherous Columbia River Bar only affirms her resolve.

Lieutenant Hammond Markson flies his Dolphin rescue helicopter as if it's a part of himself.

Only when a desperate rescue on the storm-tossed Oregon Coast cliffs throws them together do they find out how truly exciting life can be.

1

"You are officially the Chief Loon on this boat," Petty Officer Vera Chu slid out of her upper bunk and did her best to repress a shiver. As fast as possible she stripped out of her sleeping sweats and pulled on "The Blue"—technically the ODU, Operational Dress Uniform, which sounded far too fancy for the standard Coast Guard working uniform. Blue cargo pants (over long johns), topped with a long-sleeved blue t-shirt, and blue overshirt. Her last gesture after pulling on the blue ball cap was to rub her name stitched over her right breast pocket. USCG to the core just like her parents. Dad always insisted that Mom would have been so proud of her and that was enough—almost.

"What took you so long to figure that one? I mean we've known each other like two whole weeks already." PO Hailey Beaumont mumbled from where she stayed tucked under her covers on the lower bunk.

The fifty-year-old USCG *Steadfast* wasn't exactly a warm ship, so it was hard to blame her. The cutter had a lot of quirks, but she was indeed a steadfast craft and had already proven it several times since she and Hailey had come aboard. Crossing the violent Columbia River Bar off the Oregon Coast to rescue endangered boats and their crews, the old ship had definitely proven that she still had what it took.

The two weeks had also proven that, despite any momentary lack of even implied sanity, Hailey was a good crewmate to have by your side in a tight spot.

"Perhaps I'm a slow learner. I determined you were insane last night when you returned to the ship at oh-three-hundred hours this morning singing *Little White Church.*"

Hailey pulled down the covers enough to expose her dark curly hair and one bleary eye. "I didn't. By Little Big Town?"

"You did. And yes. If you find it to be of any comfort, you were mostly on key."

She pulled the covers back over her head and Vera could barely hear her. "Who knew that country music was so dangerous?"

"Or handsome Coast Guard helicopter pilots?"

This time when Hailey emerged, she was smiling. "Okay, you got me. Sly was awesome. We slow danced until they shut down the bar. I thought you hooked up with his copilot, the dark but dashing Chief Warrant Hammond Markson. Ham left like minutes after you did. Figured you were doing the whole discreet gorgeous-Asian-chick thing."

"No." Last night had been the wedding of Sly's and Hammond's back-seat crew. The rescue swimmer and crew chief from the HH-65 Dolphin helicopter were now gone on a two-week honeymoon to Hawaii.

We're planning to swim somewhere warm for a change, the groom had announced after the wedding. Offshore Astoria, Oregon was many things, but warm ocean it wasn't. Time span to hypothermia in the summer was twelve minutes. Except this was the day after Christmas, so it was closer to four.

When the party had moved to the Workers Tavern dive bar, she'd departed to return to the ship.

"Who *did* you hook up with?" Hailey shoved aside the blankets, dumped her t-shirt to the deck, and began scrabbling through the clothes in her half of the inset drawers.

"No one." Which was technically true. She hadn't hooked up and had sex with anyone.

However, she'd glanced back at the bar after a block to spot Hammond standing outside the bar's door with his fists rammed into his jacket pockets, just watching her.

When she didn't move off, he'd come up to join her and offered to walk her back to the ship. The long, cold mile should have taken fifteen minutes. Instead it had taken most of two hours. No handholding. He hadn't even shot for a goodbye kiss. Instead he'd stood and watched until she was up the gangway, like a real gentleman.

Actually well past that. She'd peeked out from the flight deck, which was her and Hailey's domain, just making sure everything was where it should be before bunking down for the night. Hammond had still been there, a dark silhouette, still watching the gangway. He'd stood there another ten minutes before finally turning on his heel and walking back the way he'd come.

She still didn't know why the walk had taken so long, or why she hadn't been cold...until this morning. Major brrr!

"Where's the fun in not hooking up with someone after a wedding?" Hailey yanked on a doubled sports bra and a t-shirt, then kept layering up. She didn't have the decency to shiver even once.

Vera felt as if she'd been *born* cold. Only at the peak of Detroit summers had she been truly comfortable. The winters there were...harsh.

"As I said, you're a loon, Hailey. And who will you be hooking up with tonight?"

"No one but the deep sea. We're headed back out."

Vera could feel the low thrum of the idling engines vibrating through the soles of her feet against the chilly deck plates. She shifted to stand on Hailey's jeans where she'd dumped them on the floor last night. Surprise inspections were clearly not Hailey's friend.

Standing on her bunkmate's clothes probably wasn't the best form. So instead, she sat on the rumples of Hailey's vacated bunk to pull on her boots.

"But after that, Sly will be waiting for me."

Vera offered her an eye roll, but Hailey just shook her head.

"No, really. I've never just *known* a guy was a contender. Actually, I've always just known, but in the other direction—like some guy will be fun but no way more than that. This time I totally know Sly is it and that he feels the same."

"That's why you were singing *Little White Church* when you came in this morning?" Vera had never "just known" with a guy either and didn't expect to any time soon.

Hailey stopped pulling on her ODU. "*Shit!* Country music is so freaking dangerous."

Vera would take that as sound advice and stick with her Detroit fusion techno-funk.

As they headed to breakfast, the deck began swaying beneath their feet. They were off dock again and headed once more across the Colombia River Bar. Only two weeks aboard, but Vera now knew exactly what that meant: rough ride ahead.

"Is he always like this?" Tad called over the intercom from the back of the thrumming HH-65 Dolphin helicopter.

"No," Ham sighed. "Usually he's worse."

Lieutenant Sylvester "Sly" Beaumont sat in the right-hand pilot's seat and he was in full-on cheery Gloucester fisherman mode. Actually, that was his normal state, this was something "other" but Ham didn't want to spook their substitute rescue swimmer. With Harv and Vivian off to Hawaii—lucky sea dogs—Tad and Craig were filling in.

Seven years together flying for the Coast Guard, and he'd never seen Sly both so cheery and flying so clean. Normally Sly was a rougher pilot. Not sloppy, but more as if he was always thinking about every moment. Suddenly he was flying like it was the most natural thing in the world.

Ham couldn't imagine how else to describe it. They'd always had fun flying together, but suddenly Ham was all

Mr. Smooth and Grace, like he'd just gotten another ten years of flying skill out of nowhere.

Surely not because of some lady.

Ham knew better. He'd been Dear Hammed twice— once at the altar. Both bitches had kept the ring as well. Next time he wasn't buying the ring until *after* the goddamn wedding. Charice still wore the diamond that he'd given her, probably because her banker husband had considered it a wise saving of his Long Island capital. Hot Haitian babe and Mr. Conservative Too-goddamn-cheap New York banker, who'd have ever thought.

Evengie had hocked his second ring, along with three others he hadn't known about, and bought a ticket to Japan. The black bitch of Tokyo. Made even less sense than being a black dude in Astoria, Oregon—according to the census, there were two black families in the whole town, though he had yet to meet any of them. Hailey's and Vera's arrival had definitely raised the town's diversity.

"Winds kicking thirty, heading for forty offshore," Ham reported. A small storm by Pacific Northwest standards, but still a challenge. The clouds had rolled off the ocean in layers. Two days ago high horsetails at sunset. An overcast mid-altitude blanket yesterday. Today, low dark and nasty. It was mid-morning, but the day was so dark that even the Douglas fir woods that lay just a kilometer from the Coast Guard hangar seemed utterly featureless. Just a wall of green rather than ten thousand trees.

"Sounds good." Sly called for clearance from the Tower then signaled for Ham to take them aloft; Ham was pilot-in-command for this flight. Sly was a good captain and shared his airtime, unlike some bastards. One of the many reasons Ham liked flying with him.

Twenty-five knots of ugly slapped at their bird before they were fifty feet up. The high whine of the twin turboshaft engines deepened a little as they took up the load. The hull creaked for a moment as the load on it shifted from squatting on three wheels to dangling from its main rotor.

Sly usually loved nothing so much as grousing about flying through shitty weather—as if that wasn't a major part of their life in the two years since they were posted to Oregon.

But not today.

"Who the hell drugged you, dude?"

"Curvy little chick, totally five-by-five."

"About five-*foot*-five. Gotta be broken to see anything in you."

"You'll find out, Ham." Man couldn't even be insulted by Ham dissing his girl.

Crap! What did it take to get a rise out of him? He needed Harv and Vivian to help him straighten Sly out. Anyone talked shit about Vera Chu, and they'd find themselves looking for a new face. He glanced toward the mouth of the Columbia River and there was her boat in mid-channel, bucking over the big waves of the Bar.

He and Sly had been flying together for seven years. Suddenly, the guy's brain goes AWOL? He'd never fallen so hard, so fast. And that so wasn't what Ham himself had been doing last night standing like a doorpost off the *Steadfast's* gangway. He wasn't sure quite what he *had* been doing; he just hadn't wanted to leave. He liked being around Vera Chu.

"I'll find out what? What a fling feels like?" Not that he'd even touched Vera. She was absolutely *not* a fling sort of woman, and he and Sly were most definitely fling sort of guys. Or they had been, before Sly's libido had been attacked by a seriously cute and curvy petty officer newly assigned to the *Steadfast.*

"Nope, buddy. It's the real thing."

"Coke already has the trademark on that. Buck-fifty outta the machine; works just fine for me."

Sly just laughed.

This was gonna be a long-ass day.

3

VERA HATED THE S PART OF SAR, ESPECIALLY NEARSHORE
SAR. Search-and-Rescue from aboard the Coast Guard
cutter in high seas was bad enough. Out there, every
spare hand was set to rotating on the watch. Often
nothing showing in the chaotic waves other than a life
preserver...if you were searching for one of the smarter
ones. Otherwise, it might just be a floating body, less
visible than a drift log in the rough waters.

She and Hailey had two typical duties: Landing
Safety Officers and Gunner's Mates. With no helicopter
landing on the *Steadfast's* afterdeck and no one to shoot
at, SAR meant that they were issued binoculars and set to
watch: two hours on, one hour off.

Near to shore, it was the same drill, except the deep
ocean swell built to double the height as they became
waves ready to crash on the land. Also, rather than
traveling a grid pattern perpendicular to the swells, the
cutter's search pattern was parallel to the coast where it
was feared someone was lost.

That meant the cutter was typically broadside to the new-and-improved swells rising to crash onto the land. Black-and-blue marks were just part of the day as they were tossed against stanchions and railings like human beach balls.

They'd found a spot to brace themselves against the RB-S, the Response Boat-Small. The twenty-three-foot inflatable was stowed midships just forward of the rear flight deck that stretched half the length of the two hundred and ten-foot cutter. It gave them a spot out of the bitter wind, mostly. They could also rest their elbows on the inflatable's side tube to steady the binoculars, not that it was doing them any good.

A party of four in two double kayaks had gone missing just south of Seaside, Oregon. Reported over an hour ago, they were long dead if they were still in the water. Their only hope was if they'd made it ashore and were up in the cliffs.

"Couldn't have been north of Seaside. Oh, no," Hailey shouted loud enough to be heard over the increasing storm.

That would have been too easy. From the resort town of Seaside all the way up to Astoria, there was nothing but long sandy beaches. But the beach patrols weren't reporting any bodies. That left the cliffs to the US Coast Guard.

With ten people watching the shore, there'd already been four false alarms.

Each time, the bright orange streak of an HH-65 Dolphin would slide in to inspect the find more closely.

Each time they waved off. Flotsam tossed up on the rocks, no sign of the missing adventurers.

"Is that your boyfriend?" Vera teased Hailey to break up the monotony of the long watch in the bitter cold.

Hailey's binoculars swung aloft for a moment as the Dolphin flew slowly south on search. "Yep! That's his tail number. Looks like your boy is doing the flying today though."

"Not my boy." Despite herself, Vera swung up her binoculars to look at the helo. The copilot in the left-hand seat had his hand on the controls. Between helmet and glasses, there was little to see, but what showed of his face was far darker than the pilot's. Yes, Hammond was at the controls. The pilot in the right seat was holding binoculars of his own looking down—at them. He waved, then turned his attention back to the surf line.

Vera admonished herself and did the same. Even braced against the inflatable's hull, this was becoming hard. The powerful binoculars that let her inspect every rock, had seemed light four hours ago. Now they felt heavy as lead. And her left shoulder kept threatening to cramp. The pitching had gotten worse, and there was often green water up to the deck below theirs. Even on the lee side of the ship, they were often eating spray.

"Tide's rising," she called out to prove that she wasn't thinking about Hammond.

They'd met a couple of times over the last weeks, maybe more than that. He wasn't chatting her up, *that* she was ready for. Instead, every time there was some sort of gathering, he'd just end up near her. He was pleasant, well-educated, and well-read. In groups, he and Sly were often at the bantering center of attention. But then later she'd find the quiet, thoughtful version of him sitting quietly beside her.

"You sure?"

About Hammond? Not at all. Oh, about the tide. Vera closed her eyes as they caught another dousing. Once her eyes cleared, she checked the beach of a small cove.

"Check out the high-tide line," she told Hailey, though that wasn't how she knew. Through her binoculars, she could see that the high limit of the seaweed drift line was indeed getting caught up in the storm's wave action. It had been well above the waves when the storm started.

But Vera knew the timing because she was endlessly amazed by the huge tides here and had looked at the tide table this morning, just as she did every day.

Detroit mostly had ice and storms. Lake Erie might not kill as many as Michigan or Superior each winter, but it wasn't for lack of trying. But its tides were under two inches.

The Oregon Coast had twelve-foot tides.

Twelve-*foot* tides?

That's when Vera saw it. Not through her binoculars, but it was just as clear.

"They're not on the cliffs," Vera shouted.

"Tell me something I don't know."

"They're *in* the cliffs."

Hailey pulled aside and looked at her strangely. "I thought I was supposed to be the crazy one."

"Trust me, you are." Then Vera turned and charged down the afterdeck.

4

"THE WAY I SEE IT, HAM, YOUR BRAIN IS BROKEN."

Ham considered what it would take to dump Sly out of the helo. Release his harness, open his door, shove—hard. Yeah, totally possible.

"You seem to think that women are fun."

"Hello, duh! So did you two weeks ago."

"Seeing it all from the next level up, buddy. Next level up. Yessiree."

"Why is a Gloucester fisher-twerp suddenly talking Texas?"

"That's not Texas. That's the Duke."

"Trust me, Sly. You are so *not* John Wayne."

"You're just jealous," Sly kept scanning the surf.

"Of you, not a chance." Though he had to admit, Hailey was really something. Almost as dark as he himself was, built, sassy, and seriously amazing at her job.

"What about that Vera? You should go for her."

As if. She had some strange effect on him that he

couldn't quite get a grip on. It was like every time he got near her; he sort of lost who he was. She was all the things Hailey wasn't: quiet, elegant, and alarmingly pretty. He was never, ever tongue-tied around women. Years of cruising the bars with Sly, he'd had plenty of practice, and they could cut quite a swath with the ladies.

Not with Petty Officer Vera Chu. Her gentle dignity caught him off guard every time. Maybe if he—

"Dolphin Three-niner, this is *Steadfast.*" The radio call didn't help his thoughts, as he knew that Vera was right down there on the cutter they'd been overflying all morning.

"Go ahead, *Steadfast.*"

"I have a petty officer here with a novel theory," Chief Petty Officer Mackey's tone was as dry as the day wasn't. "Have you checked Hug Point, specifically the cave?"

He and Sly looked at each other. Two years patrolling the Oregon Coast together, and they'd never had to do a cave rescue, the worst of all SAR scenarios. Partly because the coast had only three—two local and the third over a hundred miles to the south. The last was the big Sea Lion Caves, and it had an elevator for tourists that led to the safe highway far above. The two smaller ones could be incredibly dangerous.

The cave at Hug Point seemed unlikely, because there was a fairly easy land escape nearby—the path tourists used to visit the cave in kinder weather. They'd check it first, as it was closest to them, but now he had a very bad feeling about this.

Hug Point had gotten its name back in the time of the old wagon trains. Before there were any inland routes carved through the rough Coast Range, it had been the only north-south trade road. The wagons had to literally hug the cliff even at low tide to avoid being washed out to sea.

Nosing the helo down and turning south, they reached the prominence of Hug Point in minutes. There was a waterfall, fifteen feet high and twenty-five wide, which normally made a pretty curtain. With the rush of the winter storm, the curtain was more of a shooting cannon, arcing out from the cliff in a powerful stream.

Just to the north, the surf was washing up into the sea-cave in the basalt-and-sandstone cliffs. Ham hovered as low as he dared in the turbulence where Pacific Ocean storm met steep cliff. The day was dark enough that the searchlight actually lit much of the cave's interior.

Nothing.

"Oh man," Ham really didn't like this.

Sly switched off the searchlight as Ham lifted and raced north.

There was one other cave near here, just south of Cannon Beach, inaccessible except briefly at the very lowest tides on the calmest days.

5

"No one at Hug Point," Chief Petty Officer Mackey's voice was grim.

"It was just an idea." Though Vera still felt that it had been a good one. "Sorry to have wasted your time, Chief." Hopefully he wouldn't hold it against her. Two weeks on the *Steadfast* hadn't earned her much crazy-idea credit yet. She'd rushed onto the bridge, without being summoned, so sure that she had the solution.

Tourists were always getting into trouble at the Picture Rocks Caves on Lake Superior. A summer storm would blow up out of nowhere and slam into the beach taking a high toll among the unwary. Even all of the way down to Sector Detroit, the USCG stories of those scenic caves were told far too frequently.

"Hold your position, Petty Officer," Mackey cut off her escape.

He waved her over to the chart table where he and the captain had been conferring.

She came over and stood at the best attention she

could against the bucking ship. Thankfully, Coast Guard protocol allowed her to hang onto the table's side rail and still technically remain at attention.

"At ease, Chu. Jesus, I know you're not some first-year. Got a brain? You're not in trouble with me as long as you use it."

"Yes, Chief." She'd heard similar lines before and experience had taught her that they were trustworthy about half the time. Only two weeks aboard the *Steadfast,* she didn't yet know which side of that coin Chief Mackey landed on.

"The problem is here," he stabbed a finger at the electronic chart. It was less than five miles from their current position.

She hadn't had time to learn the coast yet, but she recognized Cannon Beach by its large sandstone sea mounts and shallow hard-basalt reefs. The chief was pointing just to the south.

"There are only two significant caves along this section of the coast. With Hug Point empty, if your guess is right, they're in a world of hurt. Silver Cave."

"What's the lay of the land there?"

"In a storm? Start with Hell. Then make it worse."

6

"YOU'RE SHITTING ME." IN TWO YEARS OF FLYING RESCUE along the Columbia Bar and a couple hundred miles of seashore to the north and south, Ham had never had occasion to come so close to Silver Cave.

Though the cove lay just south of the resort town of Cannon Beach, it was almost wholly inaccessible. The cliffs offered no landside entry, and the sea was filled with boat-ripping rocks. On a calm day, it was a beautiful place. Steep cliffs over a hidden beach. Sometimes there was sand, but in the winter the beach was big cobbles and rocks.

Just off the jagged point, a small sea mount had been cut off from the land. It sat prettily, like the period on an exclamation point. Tenacious conifers formed a small green crown on the hard rock.

At low tide, it was connected to the land by a wash of seaweed-shrouded boulders and tide pools. At high tide, it became an island.

In a storm?

"You're shitting me," Sly echoed his comment.

The deep ocean swell hit the shallows in twenty-foot surf that shattered against the back of the small sea mount. The passage between the mount and the land was a thrash of crossing currents that had slammed around either side of mount to smash against each other when they met on the far side.

Clouds of spray and confused whitewater breakers filled the intervening area with chop tall enough to bury a helicopter without even noticing.

And on the landside of the sea mount, facing the inaccessible cliff rather than the sea, was Silver Cave. It had been carved into the back side of the hard point of the sea mount that had withstood the waves.

"Winds at thirty, north-northwest. Gusting thirty-five."

Ham really wished it hadn't been his turn as pilot-in-command. But, because Sly was a stickler as well as being a good guy, unless the flight dragged on too long and fatigue became a factor, it was Ham's flight for the duration.

"Call the cliff," he instructed Sly.

"Roger."

A Dolphin HH-65's rotor was forty feet across. The distance from cliff to cave was six times that, but in this wind, he wanted an extra set of eyes on it.

He came in high, but there was nothing to see.

Easing down, he kept his nose into the wind to get the least buffeting from each gust. That northwest wind turned them so that Sly faced mostly toward the cliff. He began calling distances.

Ham eased down into the slot.

"I've got some color," Tad called out from the rear.

"See it." Please let it just be a fisherman's float.

Bright blue. Then yellow.

Then...

Two double kayaks, one snapped in half, came into view. They'd been dragged partway into the cave.

He eased down another ten feet to get a better angle on the cave.

There was still a body in one of the seats.

But its head was impossibly far forward, and it wasn't moving.

A face peeked out from deeper within the cave.

Someone waved at them desperately, then was almost dragged out to sea as the surf washed into the cave's mouth. He'd be a goner except that the cave's floor sloped up to the rear.

"Got a live one," he and Tad called simultaneously.

7

Vera looked at the video feed from the helo. Even Lake Michigan never created a mess like this one.

There was nowhere to drop the rescue swimmer that he wouldn't be immediately killed against the massive boulders. Lowering him in by a winch would still drop him in the surf that the boulders were churning into a maelstrom.

Vera checked her watch. "This tide has another six feet of rise."

"That's a death certificate," Mackey acknowledged.

The captain was already underway toward the sea mount, not that there was anything a cutter could do there.

Even a small boat...

"Uh, Chief? No never mind." It was too stupid for words. No crazy-idea credits in the world would cover this one. But the image stuck in her mind.

"Spit it out, Vera." She was surprised he even knew her first name.

Even after the Captain approved it ten minutes later, she still knew it was the craziest idea of her life.

"One more thing, sir?"

The captain nodded at her as he studied the detailed chart to see how close he could get to the shore.

"Request permission to volunteer, sir."

That snagged his full attention.

"If someone else went, and this doesn't work..."

He studied her intently and she didn't flinch.

Finally he nodded. "Do the Guard proud." Then he turned to confer with the navigator.

She scrambled aft to get ready. She'd just gone from crazy to stupid. Hopefully she wouldn't go to dead.

8

Ham hovered twenty feet above the wavetops while Craig lowered Tad, their rescue swimmer, down on the helicopter's winch cable.

He couldn't see what was beneath him, so Craig the crew chief was calling out positioning moves. "Five back. Hold. Up ten. Hold."

The litany had been practiced too many times for it to fully occupy his thoughts, though he wished it did.

He'd been called back to the ship just as the Response Boat-Small was lowered into the water by the cutter. He couldn't carry the RB-S, they'd need a JayHawk for that, but there wasn't one available for another hour, and that might be too late.

But that wasn't the heartstopper. *That* happened when Ham saw one of the RB-S's occupants. No one, but no one moved like Petty Officer Vera Chu. Her elegance showed in every gesture, even fighting to help the coxswain get the boat launched. It had been impressed on his very eyeballs since the first moment he saw her.

Too dumbfounded to speak, he'd slid to hover over the pitching rubber boat.

"What the hell is she doing there?" He couldn't keep it in any longer.

"Who?" Craig asked from the back. "Left ten."

"No way. That was her?" Sly tried to look down at the RB-S through the nose window by their feet.

"Swimmer in the boat," Craig announced. "And... we're hooked to the RB-S. Up ten, I'm spooling cable. Up ten more."

Ham lifted the helo even as his heart sunk.

9

"YOU CRAZY, SISTER?"

"Asks the rescue swimmer," Vera chided him. They were the ultimate warrior in the Coast Guard hierarchy, jumping out of helos to rescue desperate people from fast-sinking boats. She'd never seen him before. He must be the substitute for Harvey now on his honeymoon.

"Hey, I'm paid to be crazy. You're doing that all on your own. I like that in a Guardsman."

"Guardswoman." Vera wore a full float suit, unlike the diver who wore a dry suit. If she hit the water, she'd float like a balloon animal; he needed to be able to swim and dive. They were both International Orange for maximum visibility.

Like a lot of swimmers, he was a big guy. His broad shoulders and well-muscled legs were obvious even through his suit. Which had her looking aloft.

Hammond was up there. Just fifty feet away. And he was now her lifeline.

Literally.

Here was her crazy idea come to life. A Dolphin helo —too small to wholly lift an RB-S—could, however, offer stabilization. With the two big engines removed and a small one in their place, the helo could even loft the boat briefly between the worst troughs, hopefully keeping its bottom off the submerged reef. Most importantly, its three-point lifting harness that had been rigged onto the boat should keep it upright.

The rubber tube sides of the boat itself would hopefully protect them when they would be inevitably slammed sideways into rocks.

At least that was the image in her head.

10

"YOU OKAY, HAM?"

"Why wouldn't he be okay?" Craig, the substitute crew chief, jumped on Sly's question like an attack dog.

"Because that's his girlfriend down there. So shut up a minute."

Ham looked down, not that there was anything to see. The RB-S was beneath and slightly behind them as he dragged it toward the coast. The only thing visible was the churning surf he was now dragging her into.

Petty Officer Vera Chu wasn't his girlfriend. All they'd ever done was sat and talked. Sly and Hailey would be off cracking jokes in the middle of a crowd or dancing in the limited space between the tables at the Workers Tavern. He and Vera would be talking about their Coast Guard pasts.

Last night, walking her home, he found out that they'd both lost a parent to the Iraq War: his Air Force father, her Coast Guard mother. He'd also learned that, like him, she was committed to the Coast Guard until they retired them or were carried out feet first. Her pride of being a third generation Coastie shone in every word she spoke about following in her mother's footsteps.

He'd never liked anyone as much...not even women he'd slept with.

And here he was dragging her into one of those situations that could end with her broken or dead all too easily.

Suddenly he was so glad he was the pilot-in-command. Because if anyone was going to protect her dream, it was damn well going to be him.

"I got this," he told Sly, then eased up on the collective enough to feel the strain on the winch cable and started the race for the beach.

11

SOMETHING HAD CHANGED.

Vera could feel the Dolphin hesitating, hanging there above them as the RB-S rode up and down the big ocean swell close behind the first line of breakers.

Suddenly, their boat was being dragged forward, riding the back of a wave at exactly the same speed as the water. It was a good move. When the wave broke, they'd be able to ride the leading edge of the trough...the deepest water that wasn't under a breaker.

"You're watching that helo hard enough to make a man jealous, sister," the rescue swimmer was teasing her again.

"That's my man up there." She didn't know why she said it. The change in control had probably been Sly taking command from Hammond, which meant that was Hailey's man doing the flying up there. But she didn't care.

"Shit. Why are the hot ones always taken?" He made

it sound like a compliment and tease rather than grumpy and chauvinistic.

"Guess I'm just lucky."

He snorted a laugh then turned his attention to the fast approaching sea mount. Suddenly he was all business. "You ready?" he shouted at the coxswain sitting back by the small engine. He nodded rather than trying to shout against the rain and wind.

"All you two have to do is get this boat nosed as far into the cave as you can. I'll be off before the second wave breaks. My goal is to load one person between each breaker and be out of there by the fifth wave. I figure that's about four times longer than our luck is likely to hold and I get itchy when I push my luck by more than a factor of ten. So, we aren't gonna go there. Clear?"

"Clear."

The crest before them started to shatter. She sat in the frontmost seat, where the gunner's mate would normally sit when an M2 .50 cal machine gun would be on the forward swivel mount. She felt a little naked with no gun and just a bow rope in her hands.

The seat itself was like a narrow horse saddle without stirrups. The horn and cantle were curved bars to provide secure handholds fore and aft. She could clamp her knees on the side and still have both feet firmly on the deck. It allowed her to sway back and forth like a bronc rider as the RB-S slammed through the waves.

Her nerves were moving faster than the waves though.

"You think this is going to work?" Vera shouted to the

swimmer though he sat just in the next seat back and to the side.

"Crazy as shit, but it's the best chance these people have. If we survive, I'm gonna have to shake the hand of whatever crazy bastard thought this up."

"Why wait?" She held out her hand. "And that would be crazy bitch." She didn't know what had come over her, but she liked the way it felt.

He shook her hand hard and grinned before nodding aloft. "Does he know how goddamn lucky he is?"

She didn't know. But if they lived through this, she was certainly going ask.

12

HAM REALLY WISHED HE SURFED. HE'D SAVED ENOUGH surfers over the years, and failed to save a few others, that there wasn't a chance they'd ever get him out on a board. But knowing the waves better would be really useful at the moment.

"Twelve-thirty!" Sly called out and held out a fist aimed close ahead and just to the right.

The trough immediately ahead of their wave dipped down to reveal a massive boulder.

Ham swung left, hoping he'd drag the RB-S sideways in time. They'd have no vision ahead and had to trust the flight crew. Because of the long lead on the winch line, he had to judge the lag time in guiding them.

"And—" Sly didn't even have time to point.

"Got it." Ham slalomed them back the other way. The deeper channel was darker blue, and he began following it.

"Sea mount in ten." Sly fed him information he didn't have time to think about for himself.

The approach was going to be hard on the boat. The rocks in front of the cave were barely awash in the troughs and were buried in twenty feet of spray and crashing surf when the waves met coming around either side of the mount.

He rode the curl of the wave, carving a path to the front of the sea cave.

That's when he saw the problem.

"Winch out! Winch out! Emergency!"

"Paying out cable," Craig replied, and the high whine of the winch motor sounded in the cabin.

As it paid out, Ham climbed, but held his turn.

Just as the surf slapped against itself and died back, he had the RB-S lined up at the front of the cave. With the cable now pressed into the protruding upper lip of the cave, the plan had been for him to descend. That would provide enough slack, as the RB-S used their small motor to power forward, to drive up into the cave.

"Keep running the cable?" Craig called over the intercom.

"Uh, yes please."

He and Sly were both pressed back as hard as they could be in their seats.

The long nose of the Dolphin was rested against the rock slope of the top of the sea mount. Beyond that stood a tiny clump of coastal pine: stout, twisted, and wind-blown so their crowns leaned dramatically back toward the land. Their trunks were thick with age and surviving ten thousand storms.

The rotor blades were spinning an arc mere feet from the miniature grove atop the sea mount.

13

VERA SPOTTED THREE SURVIVORS HUDDLED AT THE VERY highest point in the back of the small cave. One broken arm. One head wound. One walking on an ankle that twisted sideways, but clearly hadn't realized it yet. The fourth one and the two parts of kayaks reported by the helo crew must have been washed out to sea.

The second wave slashed into the boat on the swimmer's heels as he jumped forward into the cave. Thankfully, the cave's bottom had been carved so that it rose toward the back. But green water flowed over the rear transom and partially swamped their twenty-three-foot boat.

Vera managed to loop the bow line over a barnacle-covered boulder and calculated desperately as she held on.

They already had water aboard: six feet wide, half a foot deep, twenty-three feet long. Sixty cubic feet, approximately five hundred gallons, or...four thousand pounds. The useful payload on the Dolphin HH-65 was under fifteen hundred.

True to his word, the swimmer had the first survivor aboard before the next wave rushed into the small cave. His arm hung ghoulishly askew. The coxswain came forward and tucked the man's wrist into the front of his life vest to immobilize it.

The boat wouldn't sink when filled with water, not even with great gouges ripped in the hull. But it was a sure bet that the helicopter couldn't tow them back out through the heavy surf.

The guy walking on the side of his foot managed to collapse into the boat after wave number three.

The small boat engine would be no help. The coxswain had run it at full thrust to drive them as far into the cave as possible. As expected, that had meant running it hard over the rocks and it would never function again without a new propeller and drive shaft.

The third wave washed up and down the length of the boat.

The rescue swimmer, there hadn't even been a chance to find out his name, was doing some emergency first aid on the head wound.

Vera watched, mesmerized for a moment, as he bound the woman's scalp back onto her head with quick loops of gauze.

They were relatively safe in the cave for the moment, but they couldn't leave.

Removing the rear transom to drain the boat was an option, but not a good one. They'd still have to be dragged through the impossible surf.

If only they could lift off the top of the cave as neatly as the woman's scalp had been lifted away.

Vera looked at the slender winch cable and let out a bark of a laugh.

14

Sly thumped his beer mug loudly on the table as he rose to his feet.

The Workers Tavern was packed and the Coasties had snagged the last table by arriving early. It was clearly the hot spot among local dive bars for getting your lady a steak dinner on Valentine's Day.

"Six weeks ago, Petty Officer Chu kicked some serious ass," he announced in a voice loud enough to get the whole bar's attention. Or it would have been in any normal bar. At Workers, loud proclamations were no reason to pay any particular attention.

The four old graybeards at their usual spot along the back leg of the U-shaped bar were seriously off melody with the Frankie Valli tune *Sherry* pumping out of the old jukebox. The laughter and chatter at other tables didn't abate in the least as Sly continued.

"The US Coast Guard has been right generous with their medals for our little escapades."

Ham figured that was why Sly had insisted that they

all wear their dress whites, specifically so that he could show off his medal to his fiancée Hailey.

"And no one deserves it more, well, other than me—"

Hailey's snort of laughter should have put him in his place.

Instead he said, "Excuse me for a second," and gave her a kiss long enough to leave her looking a little dreamy. "Now, where was I?"

"Busy congratulating yourself," Tad and Craig said in unison. They were now permanent fixtures on the crew. Harvey and Vivian had been recruited by Station Maui while they were honeymooning there.

"No, that's not it." He made a show of patting his pockets as if looking for what he'd forgotten, but his grin said that he hadn't for a moment.

Ham looked at Vera and they shared a smile. Over the two months since her arrival, she'd come to know Sly's antics as well as he did. Of course the four of them were rarely apart when the girls were ashore or the helo was aboard the *Steadfast*.

"Oh, here it is." Sly held up an imaginary bit of paper and squinted at it before continuing. "To the, highly decorated I might add, Petty Officer Chu for thinking up and executing a rescue that even my Hailey said was too crazy for her."

"You've definitely got the 'Chief Loon' award on this team," Hailey announced. In fact, she held up a funky handmade medal that was a fingernail polish-painted duckish bird, dangling from an ocean-blue ribbon. She leaned over and pinned it next to Vera's Coast Guard Medal.

Vera actually blushed, which was pretty damn cute.

"And to Lieutenant Hammond Markson," Sly paused dramatically, "the only pilot I know good enough to have pulled it off without getting us all killed. Hear! Hear!" Sly called out.

And at that, the whole bar raised their glasses and repeated the call.

Now Ham could feel the heat on his own face.

15

"YOU AREN'T SAYING MUCH." VERA DIDN'T KNOW WHY THAT was making her nervous. She and Hammond had sat with the others for hours, reliving the Silver Cave rescue, among others.

Unable to remove the top of the cave, and knowing the boat would never leave the cave intact, Vera had the helicopter back off from the cave's mouth.

Disconnecting the winch's cargo hook from the boat, she'd tied a rope line just above the hook. One by one, they attached the survivors to the cable. Then, they'd eased the line until the person swung off the boat and sideways out of the cave, but clear of the heavy surf. Once they were winched aloft, the helo lowered the cargo hook again, and they'd pulled it back into the cave with the line. A right-angle rescue; out *then* up.

One by one, everyone had gone aloft until only she and the swimmer had been left in the boat inside the cave.

"Seriously, lady. Your pilot doesn't wise up, I call first

dibs." And that's how she was finally introduced to Tad, waiting for the cable to lower back down to fetch her.

Tonight, Hammond, who usually let her know his thoughts, was keeping them very firmly to himself.

The last six weeks had been the best weeks of her life. The captain and Chief Mackey had made it clear that she was welcome to bring any crazy idea to their attention at any time of day or night. And they'd said it enough times that she actually believed them. And when the inevitable publicity had happened, neither had taken any of the credit. Instead, they'd made a point of pushing her, Tad, and Hammond to the fore.

"We aren't the ones who did it, Chu. Now take your goddamn bow." Mackey had grumbled in what she was learning was his especially pleased tone. She'd also taken the promotion that went along with the medal.

"Vera."

Hammond didn't make it a question as he stopped at the base of the *Steadfast's* gangway. All she could do was nod against a dry throat.

He reached out and took her hand, something he almost never did in public, and rubbed his thumb over the back of her knuckles, leaving a line of warmth that didn't fade away. But still he didn't speak.

"Hammond."

He shook his head. "I had all these words. Now I can't remember any of them."

"What were they about?"

He opened his mouth, closed it again.

Then he started to kneel. While it wasn't raining at the moment, the pavement was wet and muddy.

"No, Hammond. Your dress whites." At least those were the words that came out of her mouth. Her thoughts were suddenly very silent as if waiting.

Hammond stood back upright, but he was now holding open a white box which held a ring with a sapphire-blue diamond.

"The color of the sea."

He just nodded. "Yeah. That was part of the words I had. It's in your blood and I love that about you."

She didn't need any other words. Instead she held out her hand for him to slip on the ring. Then she wrapped her arms around him and held on.

That's what she loved about him too.

There was a little tune running through the back of her mind as Hammond held her tighter. It took her a moment to identify it; then couldn't help smiling even more when she did.

Hailey was going to laugh herself sick.

It was *Little White Church* by Little Big Town.

————

If you enjoyed this, keep reading for an excerpt from a book you're going to love.
..and a review is always welcome (it really helps)...

OFF THE LEASH

IF YOU ENJOYED THIS, YOU'LL LOVE THE
WHITE HOUSE PROTECTION FORCE
SERIES

OFF THE LEASH (EXCERPT)

WHITE HOUSE PROTECTION FORCE #1

"You're joking."

"Nope. That's his name. And he's yours now."

Sergeant Linda Hamlin wondered quite what it would take to wipe that smile off Lieutenant Jurgen's face. A 120mm round from an M1A1 Abrams Main Battle Tank came to mind.

The kennel master of the US Secret Service's Canine Team was clearly a misogynistic jerk from the top of his polished head to the bottoms of his equally polished boots. She wondered if the shoelaces were polished as well.

Then she looked over at the poor dog sitting hopefully on the concrete kennel floor. His stall had a dog bed three times his size and a water bowl deep enough for him to bathe in. No toys, because toys always came from the handler as a reward. He offered her a sad sigh and a liquid doggy gaze. The kennel even smelled wrong, more of sanitizer than dog. The walls seemed to echo with each bark down the long line of kennels housing the candidate hopefuls for the next addition to the Secret Service's team.

Thor—really?—was a brindle-colored mutt, part who-knew and part no-one-cared. He looked like a cross between an oversized, long-haired schnauzer and a dust mop that someone had spilled dark gray paint on. After mixing in streaks of tawny brown, they'd left one white paw just to make him all the more laughable.

And of course Lieutenant Jerk Jurgen would assign Thor to the first woman on the USSS K-9 team.

Unable to resist, she leaned over far enough to scruff the dog's ears. He was the physical opposite of the sleek and powerful Malinois MWDs—military war dogs—that she'd been handling for the 75th Rangers for the last five years. They twitched with eagerness and nerves. A good MWD was seventy pounds of pure drive—every damn second of the day. If the mild-mannered Thor weighed thirty pounds, she'd be surprised. And he looked like a little girl's best friend who should have a pink bow on his collar.

Jurgen was clearly ex-Marine and would have no respect for the Army. Of course, having been in the Army's Special Operations Forces, she knew better than to respect a Marine.

"We won't let any old swabbie bother us, will we?"

Jurgen snarled—definitely Marine Corps. Swabbie was slang for a Navy sailor and a Marine always took offense at being lumped in with them no matter how much they belonged. Of course the swabbies took offense at having the Marines lumped with *them*. Too bad there weren't any Navy around so that she could get two for the price of one. Jurgen wouldn't be her boss, so appeasing him wasn't high on her to-do list.

At least she wouldn't need any of the protective bite gear working with Thor. With his stature, he was an explosives detection dog without also being an attack one.

"Where was he trained?" She stood back up to face the beast.

"Private outfit in Montana—some place called Henderson's Ranch. Didn't make their MWD program," his scoff said exactly what he thought the likelihood of any dog outfit in Montana being worthwhile. "They wanted us to try the little runt out."

She'd never heard of a training program in Montana. MWDs all came out of Lackland Air Force Base training. The Secret Service mostly trained their own and they all came from Vohne Liche Kennels in Indiana. Unless... Special Operations Forces dogs were trained by private contractors. She'd worked beside a Delta Force dog for a single month—he'd been incredible.

"Is he trained in English or German?" Most American MWDs were trained in German so that there was no confusion in case a command word happened to be part of a spoken sentence. It also made it harder for any random person on the battlefield to shout something that would confuse the dog.

"German according to his paperwork, but he won't listen to me much in either language."

Might as well give the diminutive Thor a few basic tests. A snap of her fingers and a slap on her thigh had the dog dropping into a smart "heel" position. No need to call out *Fuss—by my foot.*

"*Pass auf!*" *Guard!* She made a pistol with her thumb and forefinger and aimed it at Jurgen as she grabbed her forearm with her other hand—the military hand sign for enemy.

The little dog snarled at Jurgen sharply enough to have him backing out of the kennel. "Goddamn it!"

"*Ruhig.*" *Quiet.* Thor maintained his fierce posture but dropped the snarl.

"*Gute Hund.*" *Good dog,* Linda countered the command.

Thor looked up at her and wagged his tail happily. She tossed him a doggie treat, which he caught midair and crunched happily.

She didn't bother looking up at Jurgen as she knelt once more to check over the little dog. His scruffy fur was so soft that it tickled. Good strength in the jaw, enough to show he'd had bite training despite his size—perfect if she ever needed to take down a three-foot-tall terrorist. Legs said he was a jumper.

"Take your time, Hamlin. I've got nothing else to do with the rest of my goddamn day except babysit you and this mutt."

"Is the course set?"

"Sure. Take him out," Jurgen's snarl sounded almost as nasty as Thor's before he stalked off.

She stood and slapped a hand on her opposite shoulder.

Thor sprang aloft as if he was attached to springs and she caught him easily. He'd cleared well over double his own height. Definitely trained...and far easier to catch than seventy pounds of hyperactive Malinois.

She plopped him back down on the ground. On lead or off? She'd give him the benefit of the doubt and try off first to see what happened.

Linda zipped up her brand-new USSS jacket against the cold and led the way out of the kennel into the hard sunlight of the January morning. Snow had brushed the higher hills around the USSS James J. Rowley Training Center—which this close to Washington, DC, wasn't saying much—but was melting quickly. Scents wouldn't carry as well on the cool air, making it more of a challenge for Thor to locate the explosives. She didn't know where they were either. The course was a test for handler as well as dog.

Jurgen would be up in the observer turret looking for any excuse to mark down his newest team. Perhaps teasing him about being just a Marine hadn't been her best tactical choice. She sighed. At least she was consistent—she'd always been good at finding ways to piss people off before she could stop herself and consider the wisdom of doing so.

This test was the culmination of a crazy three months, so she'd forgive herself this time—something she also wasn't very good at.

In October she'd been out of the Army and unsure what to do next. Tucked in the packet with her DD 214 honorable discharge form had been a flyer on career opportunities with the US Secret Service dog team: *Be all your dog can be!* No one else being released from Fort

Benning that day had received any kind of a job flyer at all that she'd seen, so she kept quiet about it.

She had to pass through DC on her way back to Vermont—her parent's place. Burlington would work for, honestly, not very long at all, but she lacked anywhere else to go after a decade of service. So, she'd stopped off in DC to see what was up with that job flyer. Five interviews and three months to complete a standard six-month training course later—which was mostly a cakewalk after fighting with the US Rangers—she was on-board and this chill January day was her first chance with a dog. First chance to prove that she still had it. First chance to prove that she hadn't made a mistake in deciding that she'd seen enough bloodshed and war zones for one lifetime and leaving the Army.

The Start Here sign made it obvious where to begin, but she didn't dare hesitate to take in her surroundings past a quick glimpse. Jurgen's score would count a great deal toward where she and Thor were assigned in the future. Mostly likely on some field prep team, clearing the way for presidential visits.

As usual, hindsight informed her that harassing the lieutenant hadn't been an optimal strategy. A hindsight that had served her equally poorly with regular Army commanders before she'd finally hooked up with the Rangers—kowtowing to officers had never been one of her strengths.

Thankfully, the Special Operations Forces hadn't given a damn about anything except performance and *that* she could always deliver, since the day she'd been named the team captain for both soccer and volleyball.

She was never popular, but both teams had made all-state her last two years in school.

The canine training course at James J. Rowley was a two-acre lot. A hard-packed path of tramped-down dirt led through the brown grass. It followed a predictable pattern from the gate to a junker car, over to tool shed, then a truck, and so on into a compressed version of an intersection in a small town. Beyond it ran an urban street of gray clapboard two- and three-story buildings and an eight-story office tower, all without windows. Clearly a playground for Secret Service training teams.

Her target was the town, so she blocked the city street out of her mind. Focus on the problem: two roads, twenty storefronts, six houses, vehicles, pedestrians.

It might look normal...normalish with its missing windows and no movement. It would be anything but. Stocked with fake IEDs, a bombmaker's stash, suicide cars, weapons caches, and dozens of other traps, all waiting for her and Thor to find. He had to be sensitive to hundreds of scents and it was her job to guide him so that he didn't miss the opportunity to find and evaluate each one.

There would be easy scents, from fertilizer and diesel fuel used so destructively in the 1995 Oklahoma City bombing, to almost as obvious TNT to the very difficult to detect C-4 plastic explosive.

Mannequins on the street carried grocery bags and briefcases. Some held fresh meat, a powerful smell demanding any dog's attention, but would count as a false lead if they went for it. On the job, an explosives detection dog wasn't supposed to care about anything except explosives. Other mannequins were wrapped in suicide vests loaded with Semtex or wearing knapsacks filled with package bombs made from Russian PVV-5A.

She spotted Jurgen stepping into a glassed-in observer turret atop the corner drugstore. Someone else was already there and watching.

She looked down once more at the ridiculous little dog and could only hope for the best.

"Thor?"

He looked up at her.

She pointed to the left, away from the beaten path.

"*Such!*" Find.

Thor sniffed left, then right. Then he headed forward quickly in the direction she pointed.

———

CLIVE ANDREWS SAT IN THE SECOND-STORY WINDOW AT THE corner of Main and First, the only two streets in town. Downstairs was a drugstore all rigged to explode, except there were no triggers and there was barely enough explosive to blow up a candy box.

Not that he'd know, but that's what Lieutenant Jurgen had promised him.

It didn't really matter if it was rigged to blow for real, because when Miss Watson—never Ms. or Mrs.—asked for a "favor," you did it. At least he did. Actually, he had yet to meet anyone else who knew her. Not that he'd asked around. She wasn't the sort of person one talked about with strangers, or even close friends. He'd bet even if they did, it would be in whispers. That's just what she was like.

So he'd traveled across town from the White House and into Maryland on a cold winter's morning, barely past a sunrise that did nothing to warm the day. Now he sat in an unheated glass icebox and watched a new officer run a test course he didn't begin to understand.

Keep reading at fine retailers everywhere:
Off the Leash
...and don't forget that review. It really helps me out.

ABOUT THE AUTHOR

M.L. Buchman started the first of over 60 novels, 100 short stories, and a fast-growing pile of audiobooks while flying from South Korea to ride his bicycle across the Australian Outback. Part of a solo around the world trip that ultimately launched his writing career in: thrillers, military romantic suspense, contemporary romance, and SF/F.

PW says his thrillers will make "Tom Clancy fans open to a strong female lead clamor for more." His titles have been named Barnes & Noble and NPR "Top 5 of the year" and 3-time Booklist "Top 10 of the Year" as well as being a "Top 20 Modern Masterpiece" in romantic suspense.

As a 30-year project manager with a geophysics degree who has: designed and built houses, flown and jumped out of planes, and solo-sailed a 50' ketch—he is awed by what's possible. More at: www.mlbuchman.com.

Other works by M. L. Buchman: (* - also in audio)

Other works by M. L. Buchman:

Contemporary Romance (cont)

Where Dreams
Where Dreams are Born
Where Dreams Reside
Where Dreams Are of Christmas
Where Dreams Unfold
Where Dreams Are Written

Science Fiction / Fantasy

Deities Anonymous
Cookbook from Hell: Reheated
Saviors 101

Single Titles
The Nara Reaction
Monk's Maze
the Me and Elsie Chronicles

Non-Fiction

Strategies for Success
Managing Your Inner Artist/Writer
Estate Planning for Authors*
Character Voice
Narrate and Record Your Own
Audiobook*

Short Story Series by M. L. Buchman:

Romantic Suspense

Delta Force
Delta Force

Firehawks
The Firehawks Lookouts
The Firehawks Hotshots
The Firebirds

The Night Stalkers
The Night Stalkers
The Night Stalkers 5E
The Night Stalkers CSAR
The Night Stalkers Wedding Stories

US Coast Guard
US Coast Guard

White House Protection Force
White House Protection Force

Contemporary Romance

Eagle Cove
Eagle Cove

Henderson's Ranch
Henderson's Ranch*

Where Dreams
Where Dreams

Thrillers

Dead Chef
Dead Chef

Science Fiction / Fantasy

Deities Anonymous
Deities Anonymous

Other
The Future Night Stalkers
Single Titles

Printed in Great Britain
by Amazon